Henrietta's World
Planet Zaytooloo

Nicola Houlton
Illustrator: Mabel Chong

AuthorHouse™ UK
1663 Liberty Drive
Bloomington, IN 47403 USA
www.authorhouse.co.uk
Phone: 0800.197.4150

Published by AuthorHouse 11/19/2018

ISBN: 978-1-7283-8121-3 (sc)
ISBN: 978-1-7283-8120-6 (e)

authorHOUSE®

Henrietta's World Book Series

Check out more adventures in the Henrietta's World book series, available in paperback and ebook.

The school bell rang for the start of playtime and all the children ran outside to the playground.

Henrietta the Hippo met her two best friends, Tommy the Toucan and Gigi the Giraffe, by the big blue swings.

"Where are we going today, Henrietta?" asked Gigi.

"Well, we are going to visit planet Zaytooloo, to help my superhero friends save the planet," explained Henrietta.

Planet Zaytooloo was a tiny planet; some say you must shrink down to the size of a garden pea just to visit.

On the planet lived many superheroes, each with their own special superpower.

"Wow! A planet full of superheroes, do you think *I* will get a superpower too?" said Tommy.

"Let's wait and see," replied Henrietta. "Come on, we better get moving, we have a lot to get done before the end of playtime."

The children headed over to the magical hopscotch, which was the entrance into all of Henrietta's fantasy worlds. Before they entered the world, Henrietta said the magic rhyme while jumping the hopscotch:

"One, two, we're going on an adventure,
Three, four, my two best friends and I,
Five, six, recycling is our mission,
Seven, eight, I hope we learn to fly!"

Tommy and Gigi copied Henrietta, and they all entered through to planet Zaytooloo.

After gliding through a series of colourful loop-the-loop slides, they all flew into the air and landed in mountains of wobbly orange flavoured jelly.

Gigi realised that the jelly was very bouncy, and pretended she was a professional gymnast, somersaulting from one jelly mountain, to the next.

They had arrived on planet Zaytooloo.

Tommy jumped up and down with joy, as he looked down at his outfit. He was dressed just like a superhero, with a big capital letter R in the middle of his top.

They all looked at each other with big smiles on their faces, as they realised they were all dressed the same. They even had capes!

"I think we are superheroes!" shouted Tommy, struggling to contain his excitement.

"I wonder what the letter R stands for?" said Gigi scratching her head.

One by one, colourful fluffy balls started to fall from the sky. There was a purple one, a green one, and even a big blue one. There were 7 of them altogether, and they were the Watsel family. They had the power of super speed and could run around the whole planet in less than 2 seconds flat.

Mummy and Daddy Watsel named their children alphabetically, from oldest to youngest, so to make life easier. Their names were Arly, Bebe, Cleo, Doolie, and Enga.

"Welcome to planet Zaytooloo," said Mummy Watsel. "We need your help teaching the other Zaytoolians how to recycle, and make planet Zaytooloo a healthier place to live."

"We are happy to help," said Henrietta. "So that's what the letter R stands for. We have been learning about the 3 Rs of waste management at school. This should be easy-peasy."

"You'll be happy to know that while you are visiting planet Zaytooloo, you will each have your own superpower, just like we do," explained Enga. "Tommy, try tapping your beak 3 times."

Tommy jumped in the air and started flying around in circles, pretending to be Superman. He was a little bit excited.

"Did you see that?" shouted Tommy. With three taps of his beak he disappeared. Tommy had the power of invisibility.

Gigi and Henrietta's jaws dropped to the floor in amazement. They couldn't wait to find out what their superpower was.

It was time to help the Litter Bug twins, Lenny and Luna, sort their waste for recycling.

They weren't the tidiest twins in the neighborhood, but their superpower was super strength. They just loved to play catch in the garden with the television.

With their recycling ready for sorting into the different material groups, they needed to find their local recycling facility.

"We need to visit planet Plastopia," explained Doolie. "It is just a short flight away, but we will need a spaceship to get there."

"I'll let you in on a little secret, Henrietta," whispered Enga. "Your secret superpower is that whatever you draw comes to life. Maybe you should try and draw a spaceship?"

Henrietta picked up a pencil and began to draw.

"Wow, that is the biggest and shiniest spaceship I have ever seen!" said Gigi.

They all climbed aboard the spaceship with their recycling and took off to planet Plastopia.

JD, who lived on planet Plastopia, was a recycling expert, he knew everything about the 3 Rs of waste management and loved to share his knowledge with everyone he met.

JD was a small flying robot who was made from recycled metal, he would always wear his lucky bandana wherever he went. While wearing his lucky bandana, he had the power to pass on his luck to everyone he met.

Can you help Henrietta and friends sort the Litter Bug twins' RECYCLING into the correct material bins?

Paper

Plastic

Metal

Glass

"That was fun!" shouted Luna the Litter Bug. "In future I will always separate my recycling and make regular visits to planet Plastopia."

JD spun around in excitement, "I am so happy you enjoy recycling as much as I do," replied JD. "It is important that we all do our bit to help save our planet."

"Yes, even superheroes need to recycle!" said Gigi.

"It is very important that we help reduce waste by turning lights off when not in use, or use reusable bags instead of disposable ones," explained JD.

JD smiled and gathered everyone round his flipchart and shared some useful tips on how to REDUCE waste.

After a quick flight back to planet Zaytooloo, the Watsels took Henrietta and friends round to Tilly's House.

Tilly was a time traveller, and her home was filled with hundreds of collectibles and travel souvenirs; she was beginning to run out of room for where to put them all.

This was an opportunity for Henrietta and friends to help Tilly REUSE some of her household items.

"Instead of throwing things away, why not find new uses for them, or give them away to someone who can use them instead? This is how you can reuse your household items and help save the planet," explained Henrietta.

"For example, you can give your old clothes and books away to charity," said Gigi.

"That's a great idea!" smiled Tilly the Time Traveller.

Henrietta and friends got to work on Tilly's home.

Tilly was very pleased with how they had found new uses for so many of her favourite belongings; from the wellington flowerpots, to old jam jars being used as candle holders.

Henrietta and friends had finally completed their challenge. They had successfully helped the local Zaytoolians to reduce, reuse and recycle their waste. This called for a group high five.

Suddenly the Watsels turned up in super speedy style to thank Henrietta and friends for helping them save the planet.

"Look at the time, we must get back to school," said Henrietta, looking at Tilly's collection of clocks.

"Momo can help you," explained Tilly, ringing a little bell she kept in her dress pocket.

Momo was a beautiful flying whale, that knew her way round the planet like the back of her very colourful tail. She was also a chatterbox.

Within seconds Momo appeared, and they all hopped on her back. Well, apart from Gigi, as Enga had just whispered to her that her superpower was flying, and she wanted to make the most of the time she had left on planet Zaytooloo.

Although Momo knew her way round the planet, she had never seen Henrietta's magical hopscotch before, which was their way back to school. Together they worked as a team to find their way back.

Back at the school playground, Henrietta and friends returned just in time for the end of playtime.

"Wow! Who knew recycling could be so much fun?" said Gigi.

"We may have helped save planet Zaytooloo, but we also need to help save planet Earth,' said Henrietta. "Let's all promise that we will also help to reduce, reuse and recycle our waste."

Before they headed back to class they all noticed an empty plastic bottle on the floor. Tommy picked it up and placed it in the recycling bin.

The bell then rang for the end of playtime.

Now it's your turn to try and draw.

Printed in the United States
By Bookmasters